For Jo and Roy Peace
—B.D.

To Phil,
Many thanks
—A.B.

PADDIWAK AND COSY
Written by Berlie Doherty
Illustrated by Alison Bartlett
British Library Cataloguing in Publication Data
A catalogue record of this book is available from the British Library
ISBN 0 340 716436 (HB)
ISBN 0 340 716444 (PB)

This edition published in 1999
10 9 8 7 6

Published by Hodder Children's Books,
a division of Hodder Headline Limited,
338 Euston Road, London NW1 3BH
Colour Reproduction by Dot Gradations Ltd, U.K.
Printed in Hong Kong

Paddiwak and Cosy

Berlie Doherty

Illustrated by

Alison Bartlett

A division of Hodder Headline Limited

Paddiwak
is a prince of a cat
a posh job (a bit of a snob),
very smart in his neat black suit
and his little white shirt
and socks.

And all day long
he sits in the sun
and washes himself
with his sticky-lick tongue.

But yesterday was a terrible day.
Sally came home with a big blue box,
a box that bumped and shivered and shook,
a box with noisy feet inside.

Paddiwak yawned and slid off his chair.
He sniffed at the box with the noisy feet.
The lid flipped up and out came a whisker
and two and three and four and more . . .

. . . of another cat.
But what a cat!
A laugh of a cat,
a dumpling cat

with a black bit here
and a white bit there,
floppy round the tum
and great big paws.

Sally said, "Here you are, Paddiwak, a friend for you."
Paddiwak hissed and arched his back,
fluffed up his tail, and spit-spit-spat . . .

. . . ran through his cat-flap
out in the rain,
"I'm never, never, never going home again!"

The new cat ran to the fireplace.
She climbed up the chimney in great distress.
When Sally pulled her down
she had soot on her face.

Paddiwak crawled under
the garden-shed.
"I'm never, never, never
going home," he said.

The new cat hid
in the sewing box
and made a secret nest
of wool and rags.

Paddiwak climbed up
the apple tree.
“I’m never, never
going home,” said he.

The new cat ran upstairs,
lost and scared,

squeezing under dusty beds
and sneezing there.

Paddiwak howled
on the garden wall.
"I'm never, never, never
going home at all."

The new cat found the cellar, dark as dreams,
and tiptoed round the shadows
where she couldn't be seen
and cried in the corners all alone.
And Sally cried too.
"I used to have one cat,
I thought I'd have two,
and now I've lost them both.

I've lost my little slim cat,
my posh job, my bit of a snob,
and I've lost my new cuddle-cat,
my laugh of a cat, my daft cat.
I thought I'd have two cats
and now I've got none!"

When all the house
was sleeping
the new cat crept up
the cellar steps.

She had soot on her face,
wool on her tail, fluff on her fur,
a cobweb on her whiskers,
her feet were filthy.
"I'm a mess!"

She climbed into the airing-cupboard,
warm as a pocket, secret as a whisper,
and purred herself to sleep.

When outside was too dark
and cold and wet for anything.
Paddiwak pushed open his cat-flap.
"I'll just come in to shelter from the rain
but as soon as it stops I'll run away again."

His fur dripped
muddy puddles up the stairs.
He had twigs in his tail
and leaves round his ears
and his socks were
black as boots,
and he didn't care.

He found his favourite den,
the airing-cupboard.
He could hardly climb in,
he was so cold and tired.
He heaved himself up
and found . . .

. . . something as cuddly
as a cushion
to lay his head on,
something as comfy as slippers
to warm his feet by.

“Mmm! Cosy!” he sighed.
“Ah! Paddiwak!” Cosy purred.

And, next morning,
they licked each other clean.